Happy Birthday
BAD KITTY

Nick Bruel

SQUARE
FISH

ROARING BROOK PRESS
NEW YORK

• CONTENTS •

•CHAPTER ONE•
GOOD MORNING,
KITTY!

GOOD MORNING, KITTY!

Today is going to be a great day! The sun is shining! The birds are singing! Flowers are blooming every-where with all the colors of the rainbow!

You know what today is, don't you, Kitty? Today is a very special day! Today is the kind of day that only comes once a year! Today is the kind of day that you celebrate ALL day long! Today is the kind of day that deserves a BIG, FUN PARTY!

Now, do you know what today is?

TODAY IS YOUR BIRTHDAY!!!

FEH

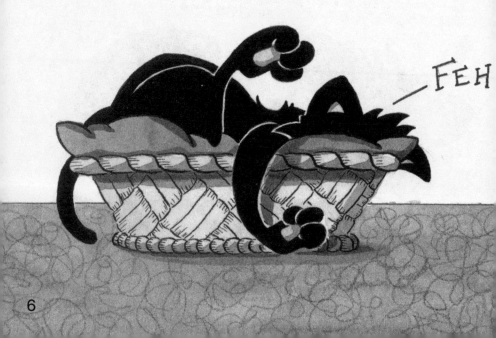

And that means we start your very special day with a very special **BIRTHDAY BREAKFAST!**

We made all of your favorites . . .

Aardvark **B**agels, **C**lam **D**oughnuts, **E**el **F**ritters, **G**rilled **H**ummingbirds, **I**guana **J**elly, **K**oala **L**emonade, **M**ongoose and **N**uts, **O**rangutan **P**ancakes, **Q**uetzal **R**aisin bread, **S**nake **T**ortillas, **U**nicorn and **V**egetable juice, **W**alrus in **X**O sauce, and for dessert a **Y**ak **Z**abaglione!

GOBBLE GOBBLE
SLOBBER
MUNCH GOBBLE SLURP
CHEW CHEW YUM
SLOBBER MASTICATE
GULP! SLURP

ZOOM

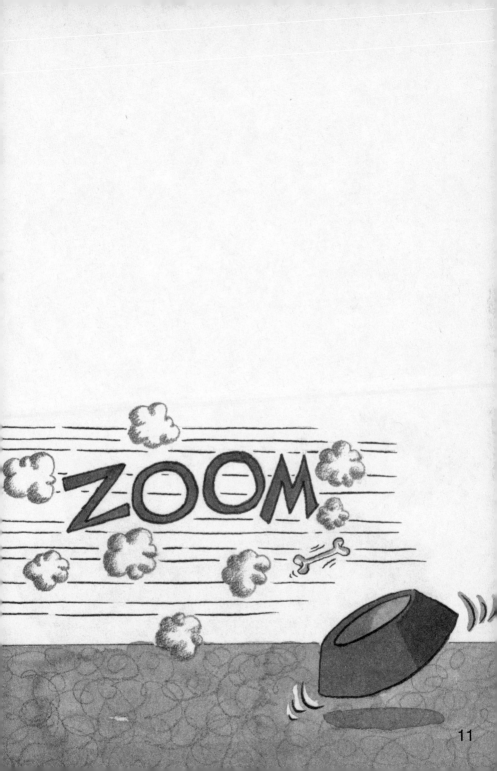

BURP
SNORE

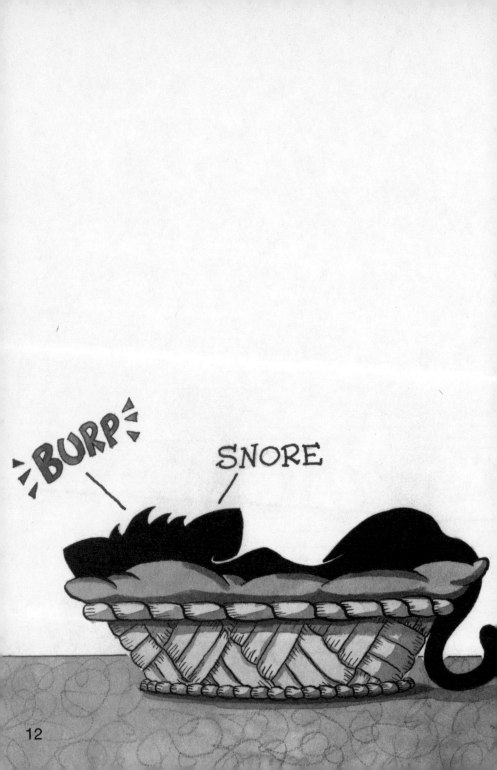

Oh, come on, Kitty! You're not going to sleep all day again, are you? All you did yesterday was sleep. All you did the day before yesterday was sleep. And all you did the day before the day before yesterday was sleep.

Are you going to do nothing but sleep every single day?

UNCLE MURRAY'S FUN FACTS

WHY DO CATS SLEEP SO MUCH?

I DUNNO. MAYBE THEY'RE TIRED.

The typical house cat will sleep an average of sixteen hours a day. That's more than TWICE what the average human being sleeps.

One reason cats sleep so much is because they're CREPUSCULAR, which means that they are most active at dawn and at dusk, when the sun is rising and when the sun is setting. Those are the times cats are used to hunting for their food.

Cats are also very light sleepers. Even when they might look like they're sound asleep, all of their senses are still very active. For instance, you can see their ears wiggle and turn while they're sleeping. This way, cats can remain aware of their surroundings even while they sleep and can wake up very quickly if they need to.

SKITTER

Some big cats, like lions, will eat so much after a successful hunt that they will sleep for two straight days afterward. Often it is only the female lions that do the hunting while the male lions do most of the sleeping.

WHUMP!

AIEEEE!

HEY! I LIKE THAT IDEA!
YO, JEANNIE!
GO GET ME A SANDWICH
AT THE DELI WHILE
I TAKE A NAP!

Okay, Kitty. I get it. You're just going to sleep all day again. I guess I'll just decorate the house all by myself. I guess I'll just blow up the balloons all by myself. I guess I'll just let all the guests in all by myself.

SNORE

I guess I'll just **EAT THE CAKE** and **OPEN THE PRESENTS** all by myself.

Wow. Cats really can
wake up quickly.

PURRRRR!

•CHAPTER TWO•
KITTY'S FIRST YEAR

Before we do anything else, Kitty, it's time for our favorite birthday tradition. It's time to look through the old photo album and remember all of those wonderful days from long ago.

LOOK, KITTY! Here's a picture of you back in the animal shelter where we found you.

Awww! You were SOOOOOOooooo cute!

You were the sweetest, kindest, nicest kitten in the whole shelter. And you were helpful, too!

You used to help keep all of the cages clean. You liked to read to all the other kittens. And you ALWAYS shared your food.

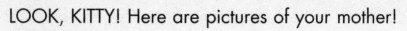

LOOK, KITTY! Here are pictures of your mother!

You and Mama Kitty were very close.

The day eventually came when it was time for you to leave the shelter. That's when you came home to live with us.

But you didn't want to go. You didn't want to leave
Mama Kitty, even though you were old enough.

UNCLE MURRAY'S FUN FACTS

WHEN ARE KITTENS OLD ENOUGH TO LEAVE THEIR MOTHERS?

AW, HECK, JEANNIE! I WAS ONLY KIDDING ABOUT THE SANDWICH

Cats mature much faster than human beings. The typical house cat reaches adulthood when it is only twelve to eighteen months old. Human beings can barely walk at that age!

So when a cat is only twelve weeks old, it is probably old enough to leave its mother and go to a new home. Twelve weeks might seem very young to you and me, but to a cat it is perfectly normal.

1 WEEK OLD

12 WEEKS OLD

1 YEAR OLD

It is very important not to remove a kitten from its mother before it is twelve weeks old.

Kittens learn a lot of important things from their mothers before they're adopted.

They learn how to use the litter box properly.

They learn how to eat solid food.

If you remove a kitten from its mother too early, the kitten might have a more difficult time learning these important lessons from you.

KITTENS . . . TWELVE WEEKS . . . LITTER BOX . . . GOT IT!

LOOK, I GOTTA RUN OUT AND BUY SOME FLOWERS!

We loved you right away, even though you were sometimes pretty . . . uh . . . grumpy.

Away from your mother, you weren't the same helpful little kitten that we first met. But we still love you.

Although, you don't always
make it easy.

•CHAPTER THREE•

EVERY PARTY NEEDS DECORATIONS

Okay, Kitty . . . Let's get started.

The first thing we do is pull out the box of decorations we use every year.

KITTY'S BIG BOX OF BIRTHDAY DECORATIONS

Why don't you help me blow up some balloons.

That's not helping, Kitty.

Okay. Why don't you help me hang
some streamers.

That's not helping, Kitty.

Okay, Kitty . . . Why don't you help me put this incredibly delicate and valuable glass birthday vase that's been in my family for a dozen generations onto the mantel.

On second thought, maybe I'll just leave this in the box.

All right, Kitty . . . Since you don't want to help me blow up balloons or hang streamers, will you at least help me to set up the table for all the **PRESENTS** you're going to get?

That's right, Kitty. All I need you to do is help me spread the special birthday party tablecloth onto the table.

Thank you, Kitty. Now you're being helpful.

Gosh! The table looks so festive. Except . . . I think it's missing one little thing, Kitty. What do you think that one little thing is, Kitty?

It's missing **PRESENTS**, of course!

So, I'm going to put one there right now. It's a BIG surprise, Kitty. And I know it's something you REALLY want, Kitty . . . that you really, REALLY, **REALLY** want.

But you have to promise me that you won't open it until the party.

Remember, Kitty . . . You promised not to open the present yet. YOU PROMISED.

MILK
WHINE!
PUPPY CAGE

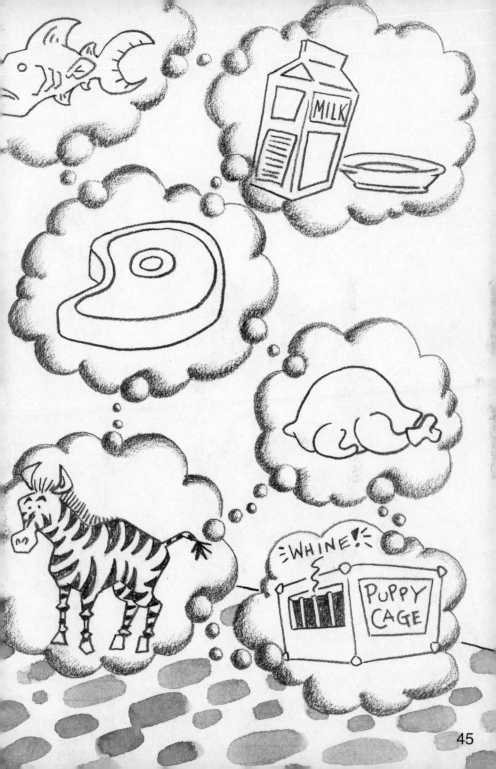

Where are you going, Kitty? The guests will be here any minute now!

DIG-DIG
RUSTLE

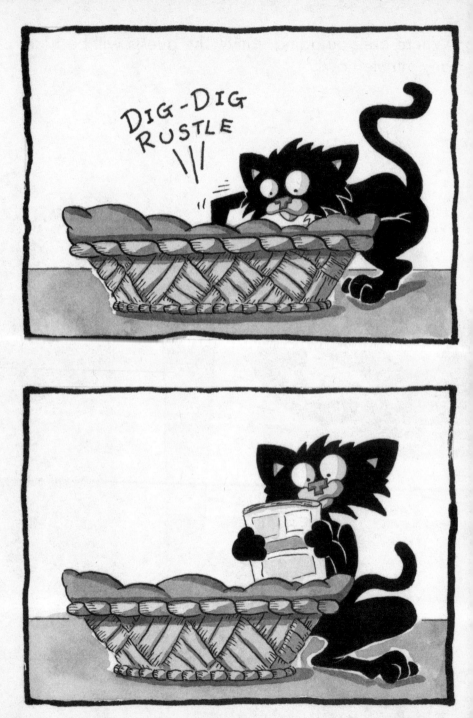

THE GIANT CAT-ALOG OF CAT TOYS
I WANT EVERYTHING!

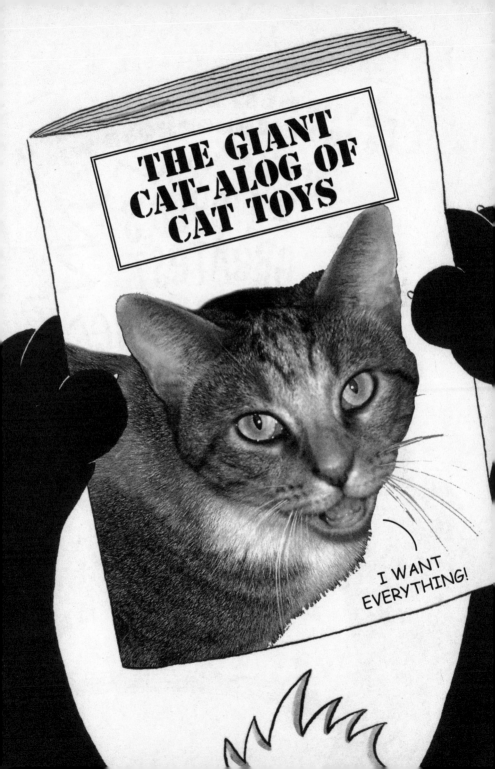

BE THE MOST POPULAR CAT IN YOUR NEIGHBORHOOD WITH...

THE WORLD'S GREATEST CAT SCRATCHER

Silk cushion stuffed with hummingbird feathers!

Baobab wood base lined with diamonds!

Bronze wire forged from the Statue of Liberty's toenail!
Artificial mink fur balls dipped in beef gravy!
Ropes made from the wool of mountain dwelling llamas that only ate cat nip for 20 years!
ONLY
599.95

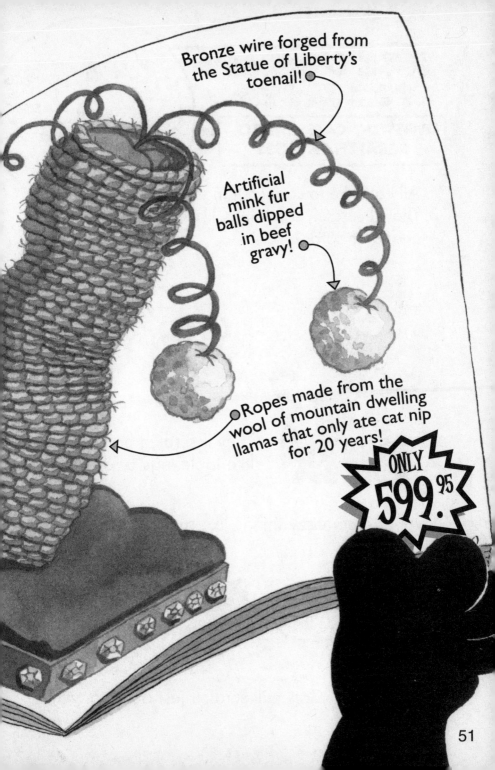

UNCLE MURRAY'S FUN FACTS

WHY DO CATS LIKE TO SCRATCH THINGS?

HEY, JEANNIE! I BRUNG YA SOME PRETTY DAISIES!

All cats like to scratch things. They'll scratch soft things like chairs or sofas.

They'll scratch hard things like table legs or dressers.

They'll scratch fuzzy things like rugs or carpets.

Cats will scratch just about anything.

Sometimes they'll do it for fun or exercise. But they'll also scratch things because their claws are like our fingernails—they never stop growing. But unlike our fingernails, a cat's claws grows in layers. So cats will sometimes scratch something to rub off an old layer for a newer, fresher, sharper claw layer.

The scratch marks they leave behind are also very important for cats—they mark a cat's territory. Those scratches are terri-tory markers for other cats to both see AND smell. Inside a cat's paw pads are little scent glands that leave little odors on anything they scratch. They act like messages for other cats to read.

OLD CLAW LAYER PEELING OFF

PADS WITH SCENT GLANDS

*THIS TABLE LEG BELONGS TO ME.

I FORGOT THAT JEANNIE IS ALLERGIC TO FLOWERS!

GRAB!

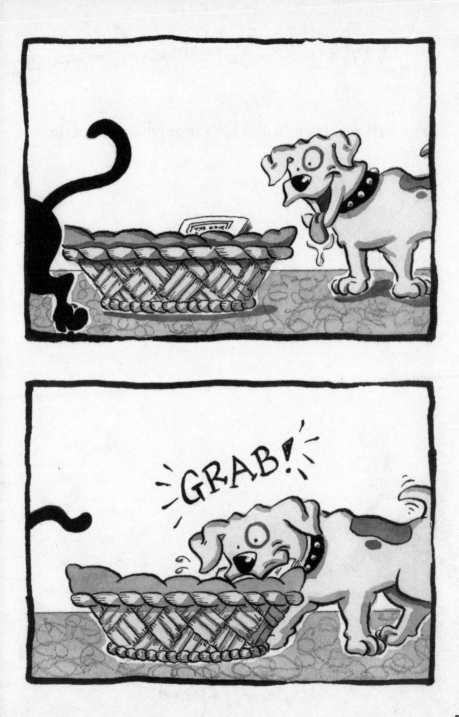

DING-DONG!

The guests are here, Kitty! Let's meet them at the door.

•CHAPTER FOUR•
EVERY PARTY NEEDS GUESTS

IT'S BIG KITTY!

Big Kitty is the biggest kitty in the whole neighborhood!

Big Kitty is MUCH bigger than Kitty.

Big Kitty weighs MUCH more than Kitty.

EVERYTHING about Big Kitty is bigger. Even his hair balls are pretty darn big.

I sure hope we have enough birthday cake!

Even Big Kitty's present is BIG! Wow! I wonder what it could be!

Kitty, why don't you open your presents later when . . . Never mind.

Look, Kitty! It's a . . . dead mouse.

I guess it wasn't dead after all.

IT'S THE TWIN KITTIES!

The Twin Kitties are brother and sister and the cutest kitties in the whole neighborhood.

More than anything, they love to PLAY. And they love to play with Kitty!

On those rare occasions when Kitty is not in the mood to play with them . . .

. . . they play with Puppy!

Look, Kitty! They brought you not ONE but TWO presents! I wonder what's in them.

Look, Kitty! It's a ball of string and a ball of twine.
How thoughtful.

I'll just put them on the present table where
they'll be safe.

IT'S STINKY KITTY!

PEE-
YOO

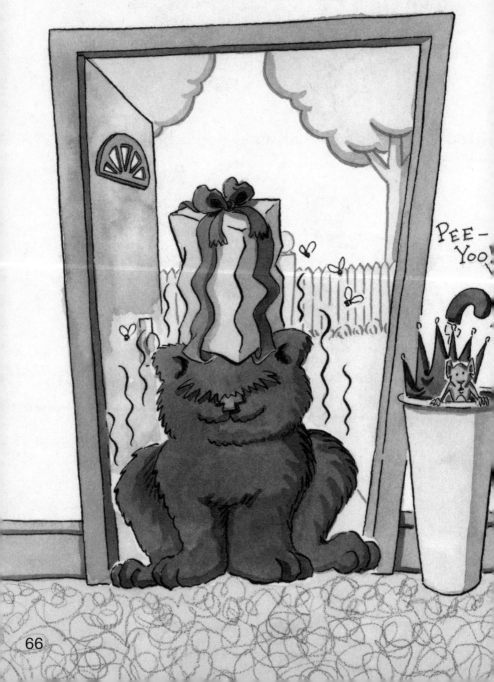

Stinky Kitty is the—**cough**—stinkiest kitty in the whole—**choke**—neighborhood.

He never brushes his teeth.

ONION

SARDINES

GARLIC

LIVER

He's always getting dirty.

He likes to sleep in his litter box.

But Stinky Kitty did—**cough**—bring you a very nice-looking present. I wonder what it—**hack**—is!

Look, Kitty! It's an . . . old cardboard paper towel tube.

Oh well, Kitty. It's the thought that counts. Let's put it on the presents table where it will be safe.

DING-
DONG

IT'S CHATTY KITTY!

*A funny thing happened to me on the way to the party. I saw a stick that was shaped just like a chicken bone only it didn't smell like a chicken bone at all. Mostly, it smelled like a stick. I find that sticks almost never smell like chicken bones unless you were to rub the stick with a chicken bone, but why would you do that?

70

Chatty Kitty is the . . . MEOW MEOW MEOW MEOW MEOW MEOW MEOW MEOW MEOW MEOW MEOW MEOW MEOW

She likes to . . . MEOW MEOW MEOW MEOW MEOW MEOW MEOW MEOW MEOW

MEOW And she likes to . . . MEOW MEOW MEOW MEOW MEOW MEOW* MEOW

And she even likes to . . . MEOW MEOW MEOW

Never mind.

* Why do you suppose oranges are called "oranges?" Do you think it's because they are colored orange, or is the color orange called "orange" because it's the color of oranges? I wonder why all fruits aren't named after their colors. Grapes could be called "purples" and a bunch of grapes could be called a "bunch of purples," unless they're white grapes, which really aren't white at all but more of a pale green. But you'd still have to be careful because if you asked for a "bunch of purples," someone might give you a big pile of eggplants, which would just be silly, because cats don't eat eggplants. Or grapes. Or oranges either.

71

Chatty Kitty has brought you such a nice-looking present. Why don't you open it right now! (Do you think I could borrow some of that paper to put in my ears?)

*A moth got into the house the other day, only I wasn't sure if it was a moth or a butterfly because it was big like a butterfly but brown and gray like a moth, and I tried to catch it but it flew too high for me, which is good because some butterflies are poisonous if you eat them, which is gross, but sometimes I can't help myself. It didn't matter, though, because it turned out to be just a feather anyway.

Look, Kitty! It's . . . a collection of old mothballs she found in the closet.

*They also ward off butterflies. **Don't eat them!**

I guess kitties aren't the best gift givers. Oh, well. Let's put them on the table where they'll be safe.

IT'S PRETTY KITTY!

THOSE EYES!

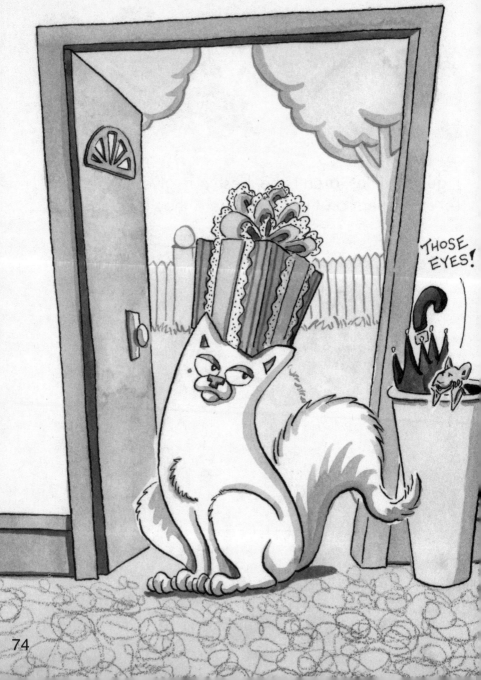

Pretty Kitty is the prettiest kitty in the whole neighborhood.

And she knows it.

She's won over a dozen cat shows.

All of the boy kitties are madly in love with her.

Even the present that Pretty Kitty brought is pretty. It's almost too pretty to . . .

RRRRIIIP!!

RIP!
CLAW!
MAUL!

Look, Kitty! It's some tufts of Pretty Kitty's pretty fur.

Oh, Kitty. Don't be like that. It's such pretty fur. That fur has won prizes at cat shows. I'll put it on the present table where it will be safe.

IT'S STRANGE KITTY!

HELLO
NICE HAT!

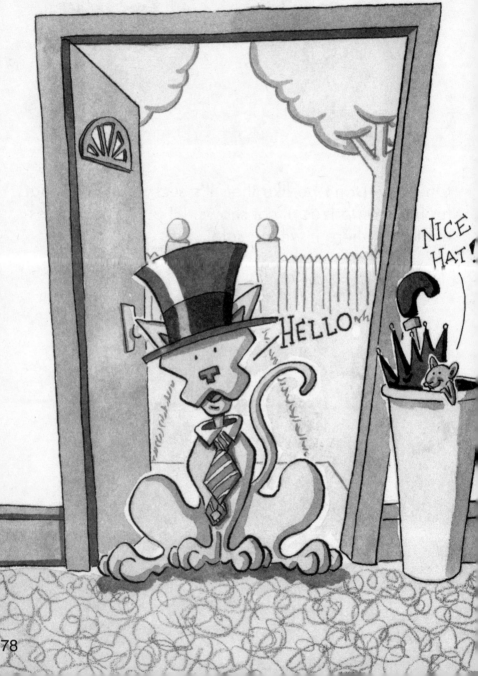

Strange Kitty is the oddest kitty in the whole neighborhood . . . maybe even the whole world. In fact, some people aren't convinced he really is a kitty.

Unlike all of the other kitties, he has no fur.

BALD

NOT A SINGLE HAIR

STRIPES

Unlike all of the other kitties, he wears a hat and necktie.

Unlike all of the other kitties, he would rather sit and read comic books by himself than scratch things or chase mice or sleep all day.

NEAT

SQUID SQUAD

Look, Kitty!
I think Strange
Kitty brought
you a
present, too!

He brought
you a comic
book! Isn't that
nice? Say
"Thank you!"

That's not how we say
"Thank you," Kitty.
It's a very thoughtful
gift. I'll put it on the
present table where
it will be safe.

WONDER
KITTY

HEY! Where are all of the other presents I put there?

Where is the comic book Strange Kitty just gave you?

Kitty, did YOU do something with all of the presents?

No?

Well, if you didn't do something with all of your presents, then . . .

•CHAPTER FIVE•
WHO STOLE KITTY'S PRESENTS?

Kitty is certain that another kitty must have stolen all of her presents. After all, who but another kitty would even WANT a cardboard paper towel tube, a ball of string, a ball of twine, a collection of old mothballs, some tufts of cat fur, and an old comic book?

But Kitty thinks there is only one kitty—ONE kitty who could be capable of such a diabolical plot—only ONE kitty could pull off such a hideous crime—only ONE kitty who would rejoice in ruining a perfectly good birthday party by STEALING all of the birthday presents. **AND THAT KITTY IS . . .**

BIG KITTY

HEIGHT: Very, very tall.

WEIGHT: Weighs about the same as a large cinder block.

LAST SEEN: Eating ten pounds of sausages.

Only Big Kitty is big and strong enough to carry all of those presents home!

That's where he will play with them all by himself while laughing— LAUGHING—at Kitty.

But Big Kitty doesn't have the presents!
So the guilty kitty must be . . .

THE TWIN KITTIES

EYES: Like four cute little yellow gumdrops.

NOSES: Like a pair of cute little red buttons.

LAST SEEN: Doing just the cutest little things. I swear, your heart would have just melted if you'd seen it. They are just so darling!

It would have been easy for one of them to stand guard while the other one stole all of the presents!

They will add the presents to their own massive collection of toys from which they will build a mountain so that they can look down at Kitty and laugh— LAUGH!

HA HA! HA HA!

But the Twin Kitties don't have the presents!

So the guilty kitty must be . . .

STINKY KITTY

EYES: No one—*cough*—dares get close enough to find out.

FUR: Dark gray. But might really be white.

LAST SEEN: Rummaging through the—*hack*—dumpster behind the fish market.

Stinky Kitty probably used his horrendous odor to distract everyone while he stole the presents!

GASP!

HACK!

Then he'll bury them in his litter box where no one would ever look and survive to tell the story. And then he will laugh—LAUGH!

But Stinky Kitty doesn't have the presents!

So the guilty kitty must be . . .

CHATTY KITTY

EYES: What?

FUR: Huh? What? Say that again.

FUR: How's that?

LAST SEEN: Sorry. I just can't hear you.

* Maybe all of your presents rolled under the sofa. That happens to me all the time. Once I found a crumpled-up piece of paper and was playing with it until it rolled under the sofa. I waited for a while, but it didn't come back out until one day someone moved the sofa to clean under it and there was the paper, so I played

She must have stolen the **MEOW**

MEOW MEOW MEOW MEOW MEOW
MEOW MEOW MEOW MEOW
MEOW MEOW MEOW MEOW

And then she . . . .

MEOW MEOW
MEOW MEOW MEOW MEOW MEOW
MEOW MEOW MEOW
MEOW

And then she
must have . . .

MEOW MEOW MEOW MEOW MEOW
MEOW MEOW MEOW MEOW
MEOW MEOW MEOW MEOW
MEOW MEOW MEOW MEOW
MEOW MEOW MEOW MEOW*****

Never mind.

Chatty Kitty doesn't
have the presents!

**So the guilty kitty
must be . . .**

with it some more until it rolled under a set of drawers. I waited for a while, but
it didn't come back out until one day someone moved them to clean in back,
and there was the paper, so I played with it until it rolled under the sofa again. I
waited for a while, but it didn't come back out until . . .

PRETTY KITTY

EYES: Like a pair of deep blue lakes at dawn's light.
FUR: Like a field of freshly fallen snow on a crisp winter's day.
LAST SEEN: Winning first prize at a DOG show— she is THAT pretty.

FFT!
FFT!
FFT!

It must have been Pretty Kitty. Because she's jealous.

She was probably jealous because none of the presents were for her.

So she's going to make all of the boy kitties carry the presents back to her place. And then she will laugh— LAUGH—**LAUGH!**

But Pretty Kitty doesn't have the presents! **So the guilty kitty must be . . .**

HISSS!

ST ANGE KITT.

FUR: None.
HAT: Black.
LAST SEEN: At a comic-book convention debating about which underwater superhero was most powerful: Captain Poseidon or Mudskipper Lass.

Strange Kitty is a big weirdo. Not only is he the only kitty left, he's DIFFERENT. He must be the guilty kitty!

He probably took all of the presents and hid them under his hat. He probably has all of the stolen presents under his hat RIGHT NOW!

UP, UP, AND AWAY

Strange Kitty is such an oddball. He's always pretending to be something he's not . . .

. . . like a superhero.

ARRR, MATEY!

. . . or a swash-buckling pirate.

HE TOOK HIS VORPAL SWORD IN HAND...

. . . or a brave dragon slayer.

. . . or a famous Broadway dancer.

—GOTTA DANCE!

He is such a strange kitty.

MEOW MEOW

WASN'T ME.

Well, if Strange Kitty didn't take the presents, then who did? This is quite a mystery.

Puppy? Is that a piece of string caught on your ear? Is that a tuft of Pretty Kitty's fur stuck on your forehead? Is that an old mothball sticking out from between your toes?

Uh-oh.

•CHAPTER SIX•
EVERY PARTY NEEDS A PIÑATA

RUN, PUPPY, RUN!
They think you stole Kitty's presents!
(Did you?)

MEOW
MEOW
MEOW

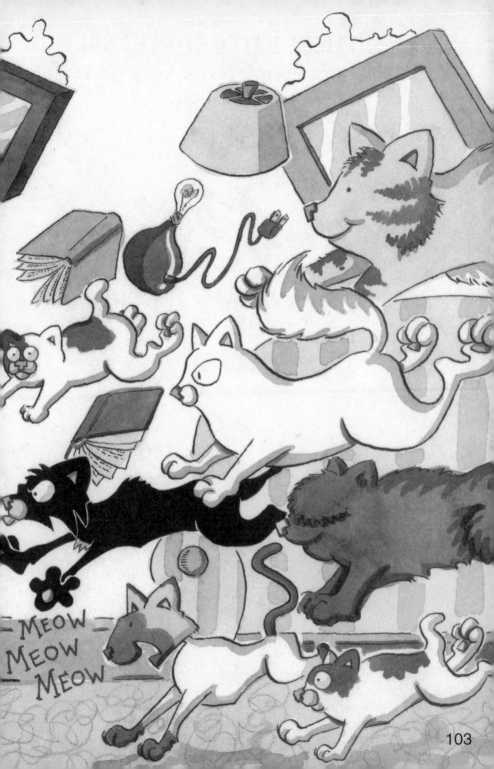

KITTIES! KITTIES! PLEASE!
I'm sure Puppy has a very good explanation.
(Don't you?)

BIG BOOK OF ROBOTS
MEOW
EOW
W
MIGHTY OG

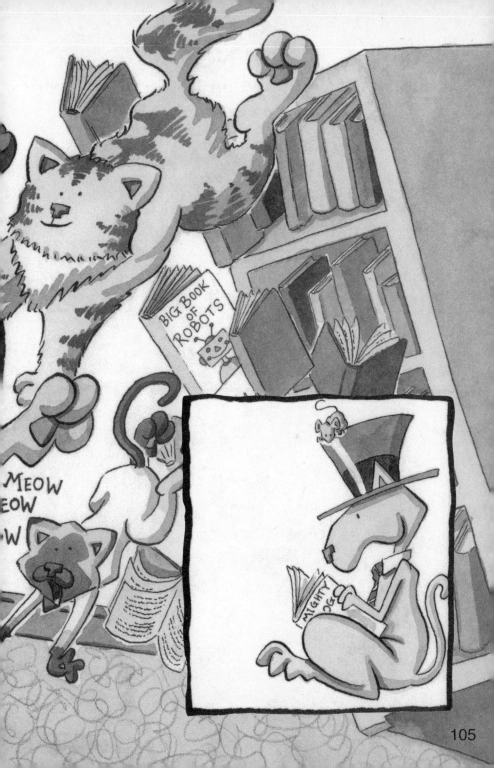

OH NO!
Puppy is all tangled up in electrical cords and speaker wires!

COOL!
MELVIN COMICS

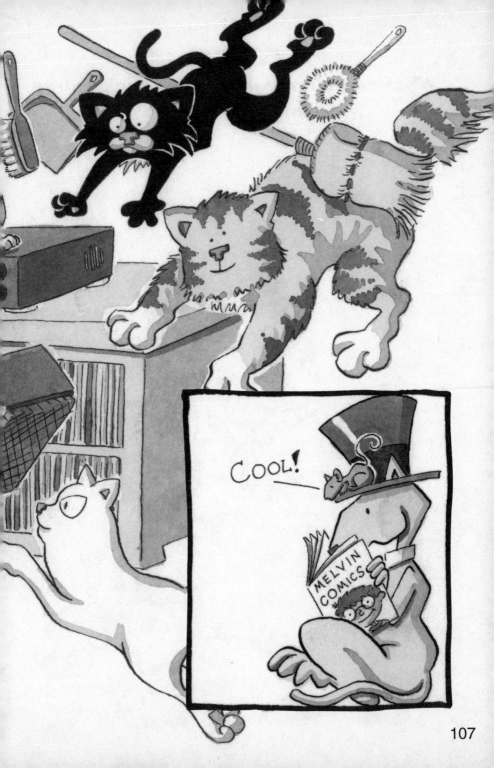

EGADS!
What do you naughty kitties think you're doing with Puppy?

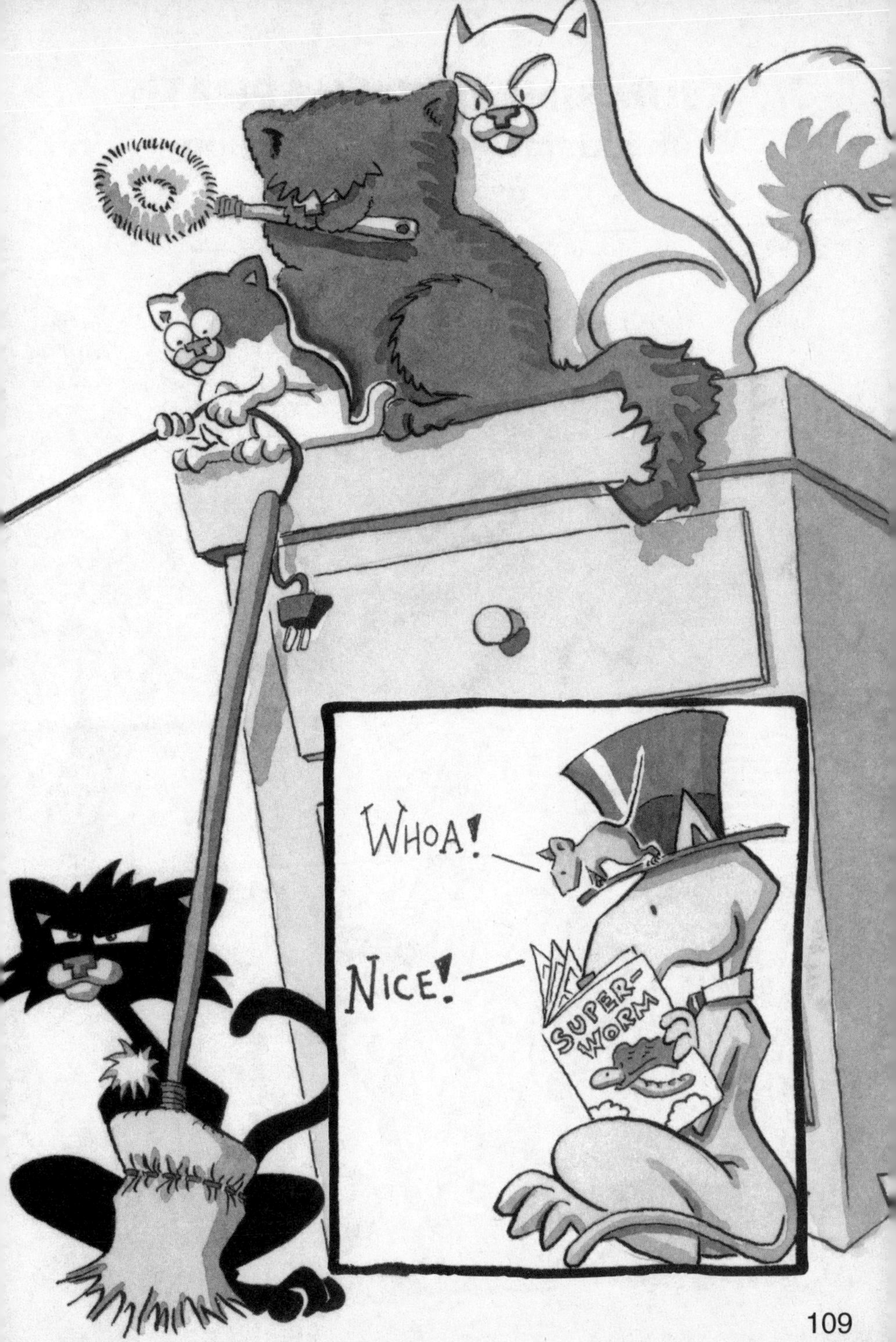
WHOA!
NICE!
SUPER-WORM

JUMPIN' JEHOSHAPHAT!
The kitties want to use Puppy as a piñata!

MEOW
MEOW
MEOW
DO YOU HAVE ANY "MEGA MOUSE?"
YUP.
THE RED BIRD

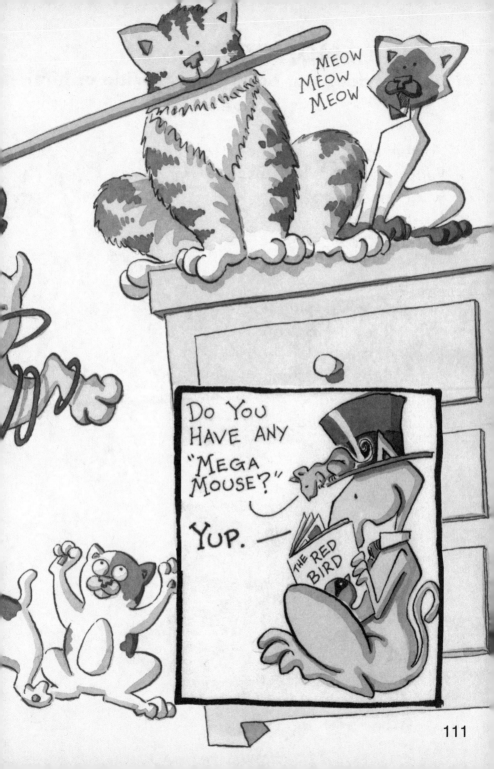

NO, KITTIES, NO!
Puppy does not have candy inside of him! I swear!

Something must be done or Puppy could get hurt. But what can we do?

WAIT! I know . . .

What three words can bring peace to all nations? What three words can create order out of chaos? What three words can soothe the savage instincts of a bunch of kitties that have lost all control?

MEOW
MEOW
WHEN DID HE GET FREEZE VISION?
ISSUE #152.
MEGA MOUSE

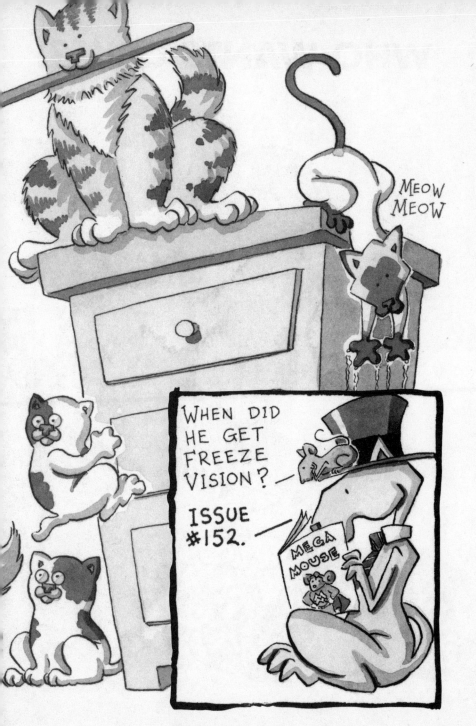

WHO WANTS CAKE?!

•CHAPTER SEVEN•
EVERY PARTY NEEDS CAKE

That's right, Kitties. Because this is a very special birthday, we have a very special birthday cake. It's made out of all of your favorite foods!

THE TWIN
KITTIES
LOVE
CHICKEN
LEGS

CHATTY KITTY
LOVES PORK CHOPS

PRETTY KITTY
LOVES CAVIAR

MEOW!
MEOW!
WoW!

And the icing is made out of
Kitty's very favorite food!
Liver!

What's wrong, Kitty? Don't
you like your cake?

Kitty, are you upset because it's not a CHOCOLATE cake? I know you wanted a chocolate cake, but I already explained to you why you can NEVER have a chocolate cake.

Sorry.

DO YOU THINK THE TUSK IS STRONGER THAN CONCRETE LASS?

YUP.

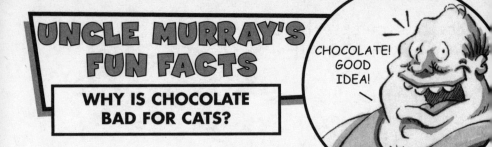

UNCLE MURRAY'S FUN FACTS

WHY IS CHOCOLATE BAD FOR CATS?

CHOCOLATE! GOOD IDEA!

If you offer a cat some chocolate, she'll probably eat it. If you offer a cat some chocolate cake, she'll probably eat it.

But chocolate is like POISON to cats! So never offer it to them!

Chocolate contains a chemical compound called THEOBROMINE that is harmless to human beings but very dangerous for cats.

If a cat eats chocolate, she can become very sick and, yes, maybe even die.

So it's very important that you never leave chocolate lying around that a cat might eat by accident.

And the same goes for dogs and most birds. It's very important to keep chocolate away from all of your pets at home.

BUT IT'S OKAY TO GIVE IT TO YOUR AUNT JEANNIE! SHE LOVES CHOCOLATE!

121

Uh-oh. Kitty is starting to lose her temper. We better do something FAST.

Kitty! Don't tell me you've forgotten about the **BIG PRESENT** I gave you this morning! Don't you want to open it now?!

I know this is something you've been wanting for a very long time! Well, your wait is finally over, because you now have your very own . . .

STRONGER
THAN
THE
SLAB?

NOT THE
SLAB.

BIG WINTER SWEATER!
And it looks just adorable on you.

HAVE YOU READ THE ONE WHERE THE SLAB EATS THE MOON?
NO WAY! COOL!

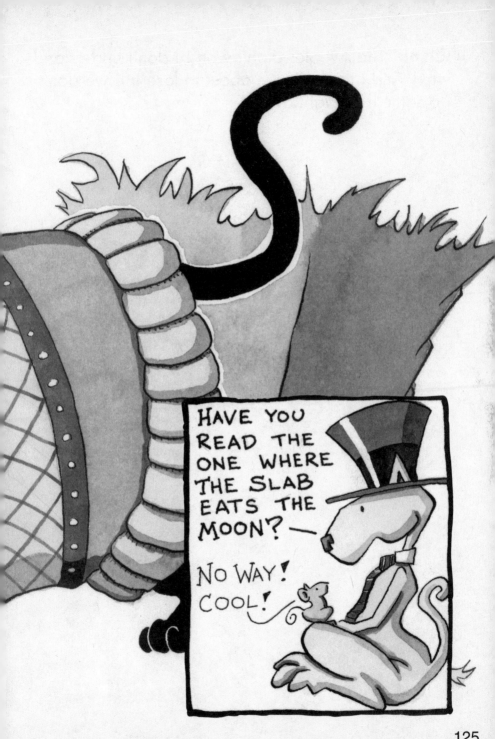

Oh no! The sweater didn't work! I don't understand why! And I think Kitty is about to lose it if we don't do something right away.

MEOW?

WAIT! I almost forgot!

Look, Kitty! I almost forgot to give you one last present. It's even better than a big winter sweater! It's . . .

I HAVE IT AT MY PLACE! DO YOU WANNA COME OVER AND READ IT TOGETHER?

I SURE DO!

A MATCHING HAT AND BOOTIES!

Don't you just love them, Kitty? And they fit you perfectly! The nice lady at the cat sweater store told me they don't make this pattern anymore. No other kitty in the whole world owns this sweater and this hat and these booties.

Aren't you
LUCKY?!

Now, wait here while I go get the camera. This will make a great Christmas card. Then everyone we know will see just how very, very cute you look!

Kitty?

Are you okay, Kitty?

Uh-oh.

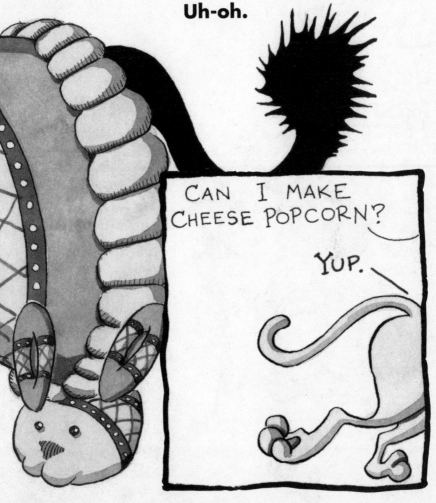

RUN FOR YOUR LIVES!

Kitty's having a major freak-out!

GREAT JUMPING HORN TOADS! *

* MEOW! MEOW! MEOW!

We woke her up when all
she wanted was to sleep!

She didn't get the gifts she wanted! And most of the gifts she did get are still missing!

She didn't like the balloons or the decorations!

She didn't get to hit the piñata!

She didn't even get the cake she wanted!

MEOW!
MEOW!
MEOW!
MEOW!

Head for the door, kitties! And don't stop until you're safe at home!

MEOW
MEC

Thanks for coming, kitties. I hope you had a good time. See you next year!

•CHAPTER EIGHT•
THE PARTY'S OVER

Well, Kitty . . . I hope you're happy.

The decorations are ruined. The cake is ruined. Your new sweater is ruined. And all of your party guests have fled the house, running for their lives.

Just like last year. And the year before that. And the year before that. *Sigh*

You know what, Kitty? Sometimes . . . just sometimes . . . you are a truly **BAD KITTY**.

DING-
DONG!

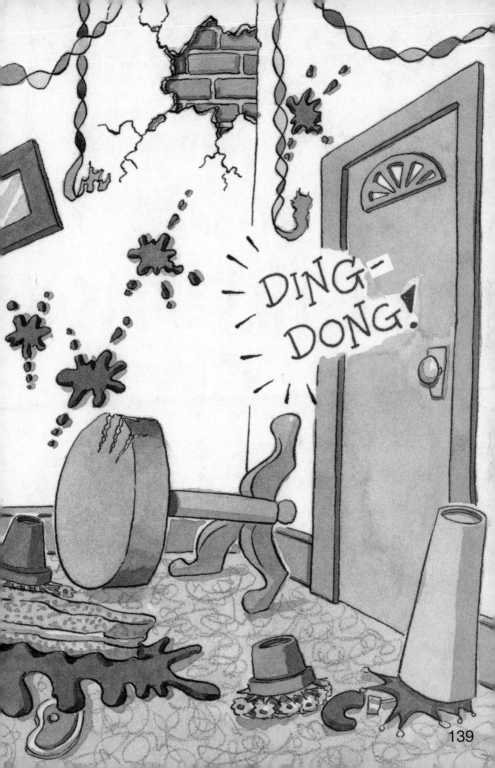

MEOW MEOW HISS SPIT MEOW HISS MEOW FFT FFT HISS MEOW MEOW SPIT FFT MEOW HISS

Oh, hush, Kitty. It's probably just one of the other kitties coming back because she forgot something.

Or maybe not.

Maybe it's a nice surprise for you.

Why don't you open the door to find out.

MEOW?
LICK

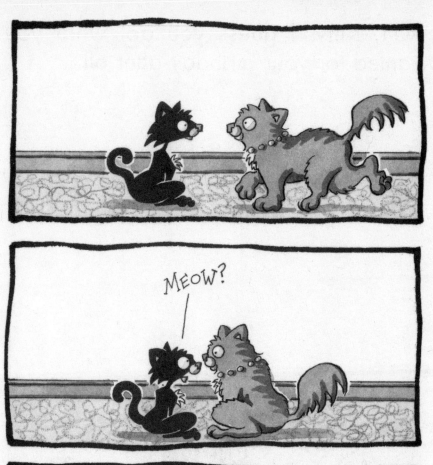

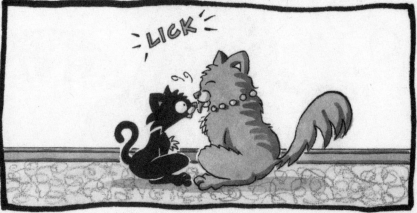

Well, Kitty. I guess you got what you wanted for your birthday after all.

•CHAPTER NINE•
GOOD NIGHT, KITTY

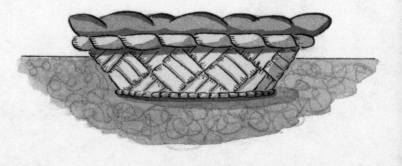

Good-bye, Mama Kitty. It was good seeing you again.

Maybe Kitty and I will go visit YOU someday.

YAWN

What a fun day this has been, Kitty. Wasn't it great to see Mama Kitty again? Weren't all of those balloons and streamers just lovely before you destroyed, demolished, decimated, and shredded them all? Wasn't it great to see all of your friends again, even though you did chase them out of the house when you went berserk? Wasn't that a beautiful cake you sprayed on the walls?

Well, the day's not over yet, Kitty! There's one more surprise left for you on your birthday! Puppy worked very hard to make something extra special for you.

Look, Kitty! It's . . .

THE WORLD'S WORST CAT SCRATCHER!

CARDBOARD PAPER TOWEL TUBE

OLD COMIC BOOK

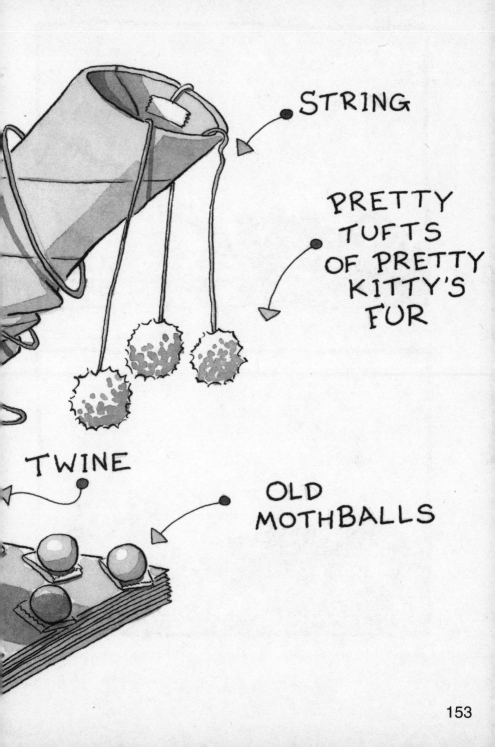

STRING

PRETTY
TUFTS
OF PRETTY
KITTY'S
FUR

TWINE

OLD
MOTHBALLS

SCRATCH

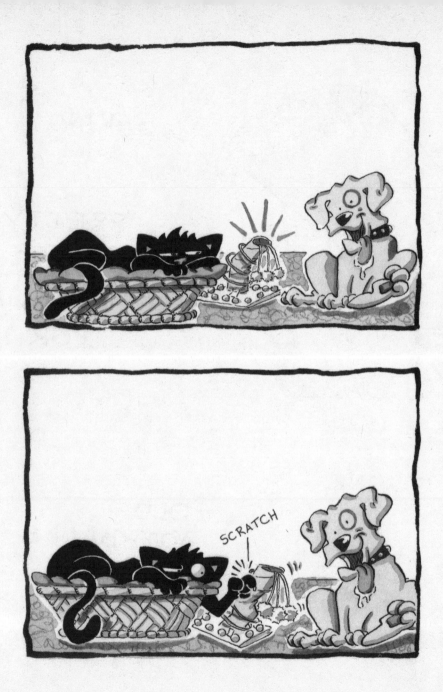

TREMBLE

POOF!

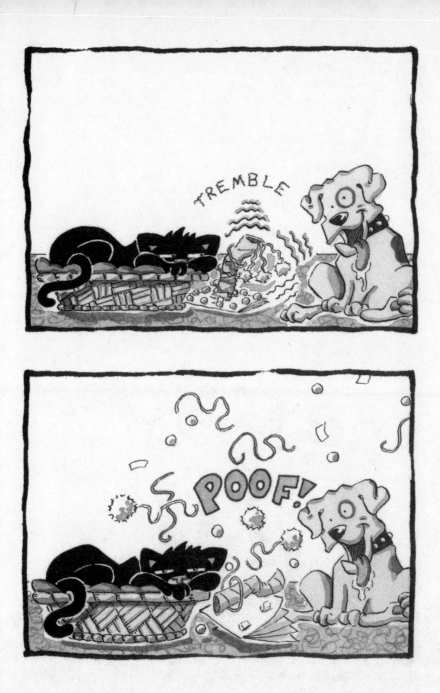

SLURP!

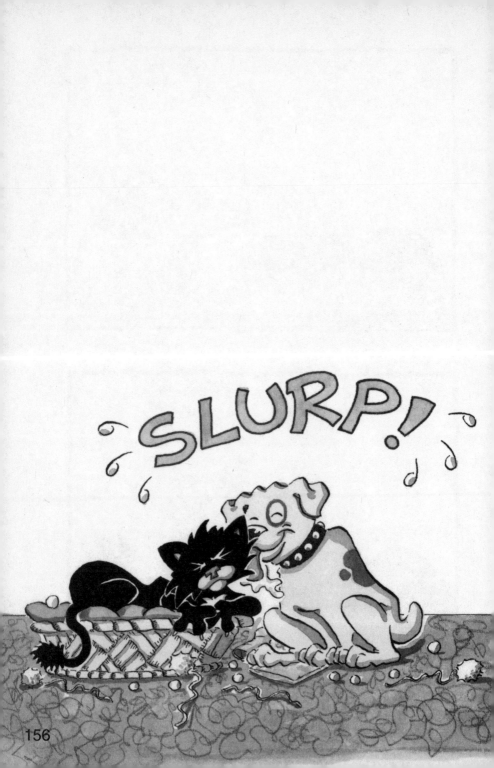

Good night, Kitty.

• APPENDIX •
What Was That Kitty's Breed?

Even though all domestic cats, or house cats, are the same species, different characteristics like behavior and appearance separate one type of cat from another. Each of the kitties that came to the birthday party represented a different breed of cat.

 **Big Kitty** is a Maine coon cat, one of the largest cat breeds. The males can weigh as much as eighteen pounds. They derived their name Coon cats because their long hair and bushy, striped tails make them resemble raccoons. Some people think the first Maine coon Cat came from a group of six pet cats sent to Maine by Marie Antoinette when she was planning to escape from France during the French Revolution.

 **The Twin Kitties** are American shorthair cats. American shorthairs come in a variety of eighty different colors and patterns. Though they are called American shorthairs, the first ones came from Europe with early settlers. There are even records that show they were on the *Mayflower*.

 **Stinky Kitty** is a Persian cat, the number one breed in popularity thanks to their easygoing personality. Although Persians aren't known to be any stinkier than other breeds of cats, they do require daily combings of their dense, long

fur and even occasional baths. Because their legs are short, they don't jump very high. But they do like to run.

Chatty Kitty is a Siamese cat, a breed that originated in Thailand, but back in the 1800s Thailand was known as Siam. Siamese cats are considered one of the oldest breeds. Many other breeds such as the Burmese and the oci-cat have been derived from the Siamese. And, yes, they are well known for being . . . talkative.

Pretty Kitty is a Turkish Angora cat, a breed that originated in the mountainous regions of Turkey where a long, thick coat of fur would be useful during their harsh winters. The Turkish Angora is considered such a national treasure that in 1917 the government of Turkey and the Ankara Zoo began a program that continues to this day to preserve the breed.

Strange Kitty is a sphynx cat, a natural muta-tion that was first seen in Toronto, Canada, in 1966. Most sphynx cats have absolutely no fur on their bodies except for a very fine fuzz, and they may not even have whiskers. This means that if they sit under the sun too long, they can actually get a sunburn. Because their skin is unprotected by fur, they need to take baths at least once a week.

In memory of Sam and Hercules,
Zou-zou, Halloween, Tom, Lucky, Choo-choo,
and all of my other pets I have loved and not forgotten.

SQUARE
FISH

An Imprint of Macmillan

HAPPY BIRTHDAY, BAD KITTY. Copyright © 2009 by Nick Bruel. All rights reserved.
Printed in the United States of America by
R. R. Donnelley & Sons Company, Harrisonburg, Virginia.
For information, address Square Fish, 175 Fifth Avenue, New York, NY 10010.

Square Fish and the Square Fish logo are trademarks of Macmillan and
are used by Roaring Brook Press under license from Macmillan.

Cataloging-in-Publication Data is on file at the Library of Congress.
ISBN 978-0-312-62902-1

Originally published in the United States by Neal Porter Books, an imprint of Roaring Brook Press
First Square Fish Edition: May 2010
Square Fish logo designed by Filomena Tuosto
mackids.com

11 13 15 17 19 20 18 16 14 12

AR: 3.6 / F&P: P / LEXILE: 610L

GOFISH

questions for the author

NICK BRUEL

What did you want to be when you grew up?

I tell this story all the time when I visit schools. When I was in first grade, there was nothing I liked to do more than to write stories and make little drawings to go with them. I thought the best job in the world was the one held by those people who had the comic strips in the newspapers. What better job is there than to wake up each morning and spend the day writing little stories and making little drawings to go along with them. So that's what I did. I wrote stories and I drew pictures to go along with them. And I still do that to this day.

When did you realize you wanted to be a writer?

I always liked to write stories. But it wasn't until high school when I spent a lot of time during summer vacations writing plays for my own amusement that I began to think this was something I could do as a career.

What's your first childhood memory?

Sitting in my high chair feeling outraged that my parents were eating steak and green beans while all I had was a bowl of indescribable mush.

What's your most embarrassing childhood memory?
Crying my eyes out while curled up in my cubbyhole in first grade for reasons I can't remember. I didn't come back out until my mother came in to pick me up from school.

What's your favorite childhood memory?
Waking up early on Christmas morning to see what Santa brought me.

As a young person, who did you look up to most?
My father. He was a kind man with a great sense of humor.

What was your worst subject in school?
True story: In eighth grade, I was on the second string of the B-Team of middle school baseball. I was up at bat only twice the entire season. I struck out and was beaned. It was generally recognized that I was the worst player on the team. And since our team lost every single game it played that year, it was decided that I was probably the worst baseball player in all of New York State in 1978.

What was your best subject in school?
Art, with English coming in a close second.

What was your first job?
I spent most of the summer after my Junior year in college as an arts and crafts director at a camp for kids with visual disabilities in Central Florida. I won't say any more, because I'm likely to write a book about it someday.

How did you celebrate publishing your first book?
I honestly don't remember. A lot was happening at that time. When *Boing!* came out, I was also preparing to get married. Plus, I was hard at work on *Bad Kitty*.

Where do you write your books?

As I write this, I'm the father of a one-year-old baby. Because of all the attention she needs, I've developed a recent habit, when the babysitter comes by to watch Isabel, of collecting all of my work together and bringing it all to a nice little Chinese restaurant across the street called A Taste of China. They know me pretty well, and let me sit at one of their tables for hours while I nibble on a lunch special.

Where do you find inspiration for your writing?

Other books. The only true axiom to creative expression is that to be productive at what you do, you have to pay attention to what everyone else is doing. I think this is true for writing, for painting, for playing music, for anything that requires any sort of creative output. To put it more simply for my situation . . . if you want to write books, you have to read as many books as you can.

Which of your characters is most like you?

In *Happy Birthday, Bad Kitty*, I introduce a character named Strange Kitty. I can say without any hesitation that Strange Kitty is me as a child. I was definitely the cat who would go to a birthday party and spend the entire time sitting in the corner reading comic books rather than participate in all of the pussycat games.

When you finish a book, who reads it first?

My wife, Carina. Even if I'm on a tight deadline, she'll see it first before I even send it to my editor, Neal Porter. Carina has a fine sense of taste for the work I do. I greatly respect her opinion even when she's a little more honest than I'd like her to be.

Are you a morning person or a night owl?
Both. I suspect that I need less sleep than most people. I'm usually the first one up to make breakfast. And I'm rarely in bed before 11:00 PM. Maybe this is why I'm exhausted all the time.

What's your idea of the best meal ever?
So long as it's Chinese food, I don't care. I just love eating it. If I had to pick a favorite dish, it would be Duck Chow Fun, which I can only find in a few seedy diners in Chinatown.

Which do you like better: cats or dogs?
Oh, I know everyone is going to expect me to say cats, but in all honesty, I love them both.

What do you value most in your friends?
Sense of humor and reliability.

Where do you go for peace and quiet?
I'm the father of a one-year-old. What is this "peez kwiet" thing you speak of?

What makes you laugh out loud?
The Marx Brothers. W. C. Fields. Buster Keaton. And my daughter.

What's your favorite song?
I don't think I have one favorite song, but "If You Want to Sing Out, Sing Out" by Cat Stevens comes to mind.

Who is your favorite fictional character?
The original Captain Marvel. He's the kind of superhero designed for kids who need superheroes. SHAZAM!

What are you most afraid of?
Scorpions. ACK! They're like the creepiest parts of spiders and crabs smashed together into one nasty-looking character. Who's idea was that?

What time of year do you like best?
Spring and Summer.

What's your favorite TV show?
I have to give my propers to *The Simpsons,* of course. But I'm very partial to the British mystery series *Lovejoy.*

If you were stranded on a desert island, who would you want for company?
I'm going to defy the implications of that question and say no one. As much as I'm comfortable talking for hours with any number of people, I'm also one of those people who relishes solitude. I've never had any problem with being alone for long periods of time . . . you get a lot more work done that way.

If you could travel in time, where would you go?
America in the 1920's. All of my favorite literature, movies, and music comes from that period. I would love to have witnessed or even participated in the artistic movements of that period in history.

What's the best advice you have ever received about writing?
I had a playwriting teacher in college named Bob Butman who gave me superb advice on the subject of writer's block—it's all about PRIDE. It's a complete myth to believe that you can't think about what you want to write next because your mind is a blank. In truth, when you feel

"blocked," it's because you DO have something in mind that you want to put to paper, but you don't feel it's good enough for what you're trying to accomplish. That's the pride part. The best thing, I find, is to put it down anyways and move on. Half the challenge of the writing process is the self-editing process.

What would you do if you ever stopped writing?
I would seriously consider becoming a teacher.

What do you like best about yourself?
I have nice hands. They've always served me well.

What is your worst habit?
Biting other people's toenails.

What do you consider to be your greatest accomplishment?
Adopting our spectacular daughter, Isabel. Actually managing to get my first book (*Boing!*) published comes in second.

Where in the world do you feel most at home?
Home. I'm a homebody. I like to work at home. I like to cook at home. I like to grow my garden vegetables at home. I like being in new and different places, but I despise the process of getting there. So, because I'm not a big fan of traveling, I just like being at HOME. It's a quality about myself that runs closely with my love of solitude.

What do you wish you could do better?
I wish I was a better artist. I look at the fluidity of line and the luminous colors of paintings by such artists as Ted Lewin, Anik McGrory, Jerry Pinkney, and Arthur Rackham with complete awe.

Kitty's owners went out of town and left Uncle Murray in charge.

Will Uncle Murray make it out alive?

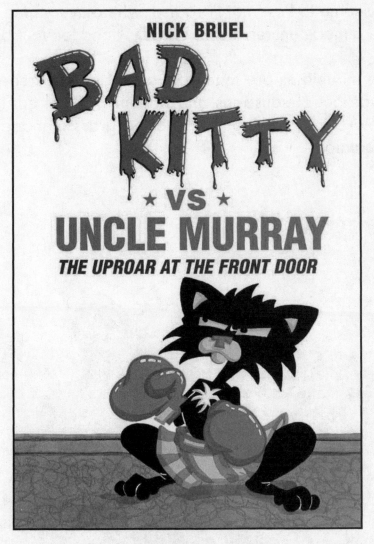

NICK BRUEL

BAD KITTY

★ VS ★

UNCLE MURRAY

THE UPROAR AT THE FRONT DOOR

Keep reading for an excerpt from

Bad Kitty vs. Uncle Murray

by Nick Bruel

published in hardcover by Roaring Brook Press.

WELCOME, KITTY!

Welcome to Pussycat Paradise, where everything you see is made entirely out of **FOOD**—food for your belly!

The mountains are made out of kibble. The trees are made out of sausages and bacon. Cans of cat food grow out of the ground. And the grass is made out of catnip.

Yes, Kitty! Eat! EAT! Food is everywhere! The rocks are made out of turkey and giblets. The dirt is made out of tuna fish. Even the rivers flow with beef gravy.

And the best part, of course, is that YOU are the only one here! No dogs to hound you. No people to make you take a bath. There is no one else here. Only you.

WHOOPS!

Sorry, Kitty. I hope I didn't wake you when I dropped the suitcase.

That's right, Kitty. We're going on a little trip. We'll be gone for a while.

Sorry, Kitty. You're not going with us. You'll have to stay home with Puppy.

Will Kitty have fun home alone? Or will the petsitter ruin everything? Find out what happens in BAD KITTY VS. UNCLE MURRAY.